MURDER ON VALENTINE'S DAY

A RIDGEWAY RESCUE MYSTERY

P. CREEDEN

Murder on a Cruise Ship © 2019 P. Creeden

Edited by Laura Martinez of "The Indie Author's Advocate"

All rights reserved under the International and Pan-American Copyright Conventions. No part of this book may be reproduced or transmitted in any form or by any means, electronic or mechanical, including photocopying, recording, or by any information storage and retrieval system, without permission in writing from the publisher.

This is a work of fiction. Names, places, characters and incidents are either the product of the author's imagination or are used fictitiously, and any resemblance to any actual persons, living or dead, organizations, events or locales is entirely coincidental.

Warning: the unauthorized reproduction or distribution of this copyrighted work is illegal. Criminal copyright infringement, including infringement without monetary gain, is investigated by the FBI and is punishable by up to 5 years in prison and a fine of $250,000.

Hear about P. Creeden's newest release, FREE books when they come available, and giveaways hosted by the author—subscribe to her newsletter:
https://www.subscribepage.com/pcreedenbooks
All subscribers also get downloadable copy of the PUPPY LOVE coloring book.

MURDER ON VALENTINE'S DAY

Ridgeway Rescue Mysteries can be read in 1-2 hours. Perfect for when you're waiting for an appointment or just want a fast read. Don't miss out on this quick, clean, cozy mystery that will keep you guessing until the end!

It's Valentine's Day and 20-year-old Emma Wright just wants her crush to take notice of her. But Colby Davidson, the K9 search and rescue deputy only thinks of her as a kid sister. How will she get him to take her seriously?

When her veterinarian boss calls her to pick up a cat at a potential crime scene, she finds herself at the house of the richest woman in Ridgeway. Her father —the sheriff—and Colby are there. They both dismiss the untimely death as a heart attack, but Emma finds clues that it might be something more. Did the software billionaire die of natural causes, or was it murder?

CHAPTER ONE

Emma sat in the outdoor café allowing the sun to keep her warm even though it was a cool, comfortable February day. Still, she was glad she wore the extra sweater. Keeping the core warm helped to keep the extremities warm, or so her dad taught her. She was happy to not have to wear jeans or slacks but could wear a nice skirt to match her top instead. And the clear sky overhead helped her feel confident in her classy heels since she didn't need to worry about rain or snow. She wanted to look pretty. Even though Colby might not be her official Valentine, if she ran into him today, she hoped he'd be impressed, too.

She waited for her best friend Rachel, and they chose this café for the outdoor area that allowed for

Molly, Emma's foster puppy, to stay with her. The pair hadn't met up for coffee in a while, though texting meant that keeping in touch was not an issue. It was a little before ten a.m. and Emma spotted Rachel and waved her over to the table the moment she approached.

Rachel smiled, and set her designer purse on the stone table in front of her. "I haven't had a decent latte in weeks. This place is amazing. We should come here more often."

"Oh, I know, right? They have the best macchiatos!" Emma agreed. Molly stood up and wagged her giant tail back and forth in a bit of excitement.

Rachel stooped down in her business casual slacks and scratched the Saint Bernard puppy behind the ears. Pleased with the greeting, Molly laid back down as the two ladies sat as well. The waiter stopped in and took their orders quickly before leaving them alone for a moment.

"So, Thomas told me he wanted chocolates for Valentine's, and I said that he should bring me chocolates instead," Rachel joked.

"He's so funny. How are you guys? I saw those hiking pics on your profile. The ones from last weekend." Emma smiled as the waiter came with their coffees and set them on the table along with the dessert sampler they had ordered.

"We're great. Thomas is doing much better now that he's getting out of the house more. I still can't get him to go everywhere, but he's loosened up a lot."

"That's good! Maybe you should take him on one of your business trips?"

"I ask him all the time," Rachel said, frowning into her coffee before taking a sip in the pause, "but he always comes up with a good reason not to go."

"Have you tried 'accidentally' bringing him along?" Emma raised an eyebrow at her friend.

"Not really. I'm not sure I can make that work," Rachel's brows scrunched.

"Sometimes I 'accidentally' find myself in situations where Colby is working. I don't know, maybe it's just my luck that does that."

"I don't know... you're very clever. I doubt it's 'accidental' at all," Rachel joked, picking up a fork and checking out the desserts on their shared platter.

"Maybe, maybe not!"

They both laughed.

"This place makes great desserts," Rachel said around a bite of chocolate cheesecake.

"They make chocolates, too... if you want to get some for Thomas after all."

Rachel's eyes widened, "Really?"

They ordered a sample platter of the assorted chocolates they had in the shop as well. Molly, Emma's dog, twitched in her sleep at Emma's feet, causing Emma to reach down and comfort the puppy with a pat before choosing a chocolate to try. The two ladies worked on the sweets and tried explaining the delicate flavors contained inside each of the chocolate candies. Some were salty while others were extra sweet. Emma left the spicy one for Rachel. She guessed her friend wouldn't mind.

"And how is it going between you and Colby?" Rachel asked, thankfully avoiding eye contact with Emma.

Emma sighed. "There's not much going on there. I keep trying to get him to notice me, but he doesn't seem to think of me as much more than the same little fourteen-year-old kid I was when we met. It's like he doesn't notice I'm twenty now."

"He'll come around." Rachel laughed. "Men are just oblivious. You have to be really obvious about your feelings for him in order for him to take notice. Have you made the first move yet?"

Heat rose in Emma's cheeks. She hadn't realized

how nervous she was about the thought of making the first move until then. "I haven't asked or told him anything yet. I'm waiting for him to show me that he's also interested."

Molly raised her head to the sky, graciously accepting a pat on the head. It was amazing that the gentle pat could help calm Emma's nerves so easily.

"You know, they need more pet-friendly shops like this one. Could you imagine?" Rachel seemed to notice Emma's reservations and changed the subject.

"That would be amazing. I could take Molly everywhere!" She smiled down at the puppy "Isn't that right, Mal-Mal?"

"You know, maybe you should look into training Molly as a therapy dog, then she really could go everywhere with you. And her calm temperament would be ideal for that."

Emma blinked. "That's not a bad idea, actually I was—"

A cell phone ring interrupted their conversation. Emma reached for her phone. The old-fashioned ringtone made it stand out, so she knew it was hers.

"You haven't changed your ringtone? How long have you had your phone?" Rachel joked.

"I just didn't like the other sounds. This one is

mine, hush." Emma laughed before answering the call. On the line was Emma's boss, Dr. Lawrence.

Emma watched Rachel whisper to the waiter while pointing to chocolates on the tray while Dr. Lawrence spoke. "Emma, I need you to go up to the Van Horn's place. Do you know how to get there?"

"I'm pretty sure I do." Emma nodded even though the doctor couldn't see her. "But if not, I've got GPS."

"Great. The dispatcher called and said there was a problem at the Van Horn estate."

"Oh, no. I hope everything is okay."

"Yes, I do too. The elder Mrs. Van Horn's cat, Julius, is a regular patient of ours. We want to check him over and give him a place to stay until whatever the situation is at the estate. Your father's dispatcher called us to let us know."

"Oh... no," Emma hesitated. She was allergic to some cats and fine with others, so she tried to avoid them all whenever possible.

"You should be fine. The cat should already be in a carrier when you arrive."

After heaving a big sigh, Emma said, "Okay, I'll get it done right away."

Then she remembered that if her father was at the Van Horn's place, maybe Colby would be too.

Although it was a tragic reason to see Colby, she still had a little flutter of butterflies in her stomach at the thought that he'd be there. She hit the end button on her phone before slipping it back into her purse.

"Duty calls. I have to go to the Van Horn's place. Apparently, their cat needs retrieving." Emma sighed. "Are you allergic to cats? Some seem to affect me horribly, but others I'm fine with."

"I don't think I am? I didn't know you were allergic?" Rachel empathized.

"Yea, I love cats. I guess my body doesn't." She laughed and started up from the table. Molly stood at attention with her.

"Do you have gloves or something?" Rachel asked and stood as well.

"No, but Dr. Lawrence says the cat should be in a tote." Emma sighed. "I just have to be near cat dander and my sinuses go off."

She waved in the direction of the waiter, but Rachel pushed down her hand. "I already paid. My treat this time. You get it next time."

It warmed Emma's heart, and she offered her friend a wide smile. "Did you order Thomas any chocolates?"

"I got him the spicy chili ones. I'm sure he'll love

them!" Lifting an eyebrow, a sinister look sparkled in Rachel's eye as she laughed.

Emma laughed, too, leading Molly to her car. "Hope he likes spicy food."

Rachel waved, holding the bag of chocolates and starting for her own vehicle. "He does!"

The two laughed and headed in their separate directions. Emma opened the hatch to the back of her SUV, and Molly hopped in obediently. She sure was smart for a five-month-old puppy. *Were all Saint Bernard dogs like this?* She made a mental note to look into therapy training for dogs as she pushed the hatch closed and started for the driver's side of the truck. It wasn't too far to the Van Horn estate, and her stomach fluttered again when she thought she might get to see Colby.

CHAPTER TWO

Being the wealthiest residents of Ridgeway, the Van Horn's estate stood at the top of a hill. Emma navigated the long driveway that led up to the amazingly beautiful mansion. The design of the home's brick structure and the property's gardening were extraordinarily well kept. Emma parked her SUV near the east side of the home, away from the driveway, unsure whether to bring the Saint Bernard. After eyeing the yard behind the property, Emma decided to leave Molly in the vehicle. Molly would have been a handful with that much playroom. Emma checked her phone for missed calls before cracking a window and filling up a bowl with water. She pet Molly and the dog returned her kindness with a few licks on her palm before she shut the door.

This was just a pet emergency, as the elder Van Horn lived alone in the mansion as far as Emma knew. The huge structure made her feel a bit nervous. Would she find her father easily in the big place, or get lost? Despite her nervousness, the job was simple. She needed to retrieve a cat and take it back to Dr. Lawrence. She had her objective. Emma told herself repeatedly that cats are nice and it's not the cat's fault she's allergic. The Van Horn's cat just needed a ride to the vet. She hoped nothing would go wrong.

Emma walked from one side of the house to the other, surveying it as her dad had taught her. Any time she would go with him on a call to a house, one of the first things to do is secure the location and check for any signs of a break in. The mixture of soft yard and gravel around the property made walking in heels awkward and painful. The mansion was huge. It had at least six bedrooms. Emma didn't notice any broken windows or objects out of place. However, she did see home security cameras peeking through a few of the windows. They weren't hidden very well.

Finding standard yard equipment and the

home's fire logs all arranged normally, everything checked out okay. As she made her way to the front door, Emma noticed the Van Horn's entrance was missing a deadbolt. The handle on the door was just a normal latch but there was not a second lock. Most doors had two locks, one in the handle and one in the deadbolt. This door had neither. Only the latch handle was visible. *That's strange.*

Tugging on the door, Emma couldn't open it. The handle and its lever were depressed correctly, but the door was stuck shut. Emma stepped back, refusing to try harder and possibly break the door. Then she skirted around the house, peering in windows looking for the Sheriff or the cat. She rounded the west side of the house and nearly collided with a woman walking in the opposite direction.

"Oh gosh! I'm so sorry! You scared me," the woman said, shaking off the adrenaline from the encounter.

"Oh no! My apologies! I didn't mean to startle you!" Emma said.

"Are you visiting?" the girl asked. She was about four or five inches shorter than Emma was, even though she wore heels. Her hair style and clothing were similar in style to Emma's which made her almost feel that the shorter, stocky woman might be the same age as her but the wrinkles in the corners of her eyes suggested she was a few years older.

"I work with Dr. Lawrence, the town vet. He sent me here for an emergency collection," Emma replied.

"An emergency? What's wrong?" The girl's eyes grew wide under her red framed glasses.

"I'm not sure. Apparently, there's a cat around here somewhere. My name is Emma by the way. Are you a Van Horn?" Emma wanted to make sure she wasn't talking to a random stranger on the property.

"Yes, my name is Denise. This is my aunt's house. I just stopped by to pick her up for a shareholder's meeting in Richmond this afternoon."

Emma's heart sank. Denise Van Horn spoke as if she didn't know about her aunt yet. Emma swallowed. She knew it was standard procedure to let her father handle that situation, but she felt guilty for remaining silent about it. Before she could say a word, Denise said, "Well, let's get inside. If you're here for the cat, I'm sure my aunt must be waiting for you."

Awkward. But Emma stayed silent again instead of correcting her. The two walked toward the front door and Emma found her tongue. "I think the front door is broken. It wouldn't open and was stuck when I tried it."

Denise laughed. "I know why you might think that. You might not have ever seen this kind of door before. My aunt was ahead of her time. Our family business is in home security. The kind of lock on the door is actually a biometric scanner which only unlocks the door for an authorized palm scan."

Emma blinked. It all sounded like a sci-fi novel. In Ridgeway? "For real?"

Denise nodded with another laugh as she stepped up to the door and demonstrated how it worked.

"You have to put your palm here." She placed her hand over a slightly discolored brick next to the door frame. "It scans your hand and unlocks the door."

After a click and a beep, the door unlatched and opened an inch or so before Denise even grabbed hold of the handle.

"Wow! That's amazing!" Emma internalized her questions of how it might work if the power were to go out. Sometimes her mind shot in directions she knew were better kept to herself. Her father taught her that you often learn more by listening than by asking questions before the victim or culprit is done giving up information. And Denise wasn't quite finished yet.

The short, stocky woman stepped into the foyer of the house and further explained how her aunt's whole home was utilizing the latest and greatest security products which her family's business produced and marketed to the masses. Among the features were a programmable biometric scanner, window frames with open detection built in, and a smart home system that automatically regulated the home air conditioning using thermal results from the many cameras installed. As if Denise were a walking advertisement, she mentioned that "Van Horn Security does not sell the A/C unit, but they do sell the technology to use it properly."

Laughing on her way into the house, Emma's attention was drawn immediately to the clop-clop of her high heels on the wooden floor. Her ankles were sore from walking through the terrain outside. Her head swiveled for a moment as she absorbed the magnitude of the home. So much money was spent on the house and its furnishings, so it made sense that the Van Horns would have used their own security system. The beautiful artwork hung in the main foyer could likely have sold for the same price the family purchased the land for.

Emma kept her attention focused on finding the cat. The Sheriff was always present when there were troubling events in the town. It was strange she didn't see his patrol car out front, which reinforced her idea that maybe the cat was the only emergency. She also kept her eyes peeled for him just in case. Denise and Emma continued their tour of the house, checking out each room around the main floor while observing the technology spread around the home with all the promises of security.

"The coolest thing, I think, is the automatic thermostat. No matter which room you're in, all you have to do is set the temperature you want, and it stays that way." Denise smiled. "Even if it's a blizzard outside, the house will be the perfect temperature. Warm and cozy."

"That sounds amazing. I usually have three blankets and my pajamas to keep me warm," Emma joked. They saw the living room and the guest bedroom before making their way to the main hall again.

Oddly, Colby was standing at the end of the corridor. Emma's heart leapt and she blinked twice to make sure she wasn't imagining it. He ran a hand through his sandy brown hair, as his ball cap was snapped onto a belt loop on his side. Always the gentleman, he'd never wear a hat indoors. His green eyes flashed in their direction as they approached.

Denise didn't seem terribly surprised. "Hello there, officer. Did my aunt call you out today to check the system?"

Colby blinked when he saw Emma. Dismissing Denise for a moment, the frustrated K9 officer sighed and asked, "What are you doing here, Emma. This is a crime scene. And who is this with you?"

"Crime scene?" Denise blinked, her smile faltering a moment.

Emma's eyes flashed toward the bedroom Colby stood in front of and she spotted her father. "Dad?" she called out.

He stood in front of the large bed and when he turned toward the sound of her voice, the body on the bed was exposed. Mrs. Van Horn lay there, motionless. Eyes still closed, she still appeared to be asleep but for the blueish pallor of her skin.

Denise shrieked and rushed into the room. "Aunt Elaine!"

The sheriff growled. "Colby, dang it. Why are there people here? I told you not to let anyone in!" He caught Denise in his arms before she could touch anything and nodded toward Colby. "Get them out of here; I'm trying to figure this mess out!"

Denise whimpered and started panicking, lunging for the room where her deceased Aunt lay. "No! This can't be happening. NO!"

The two men combined forces to calm Denise. Meanwhile they herded her toward the door. The poor girl was horrified at the sight of her aunt motionless on the bed. Once everyone was ushered out in the hallway, Emma's father glared at Colby, returned to the bedroom and shut the door.

"What happened? Why is she like that?" Denise hollered at the closed door.

"Ma'am, please calm down. You're family of the deceased?" Colby asked, his eyes infused with sympathy.

"Deceased? My aunt's really gone?" Denise's voice cracked.

Colby nodded, a grave look on his features. "I'm afraid it appears your aunt had a heart attack. She died in her sleep."

Looking down, Denise really started to freak out. "This can't be happening. What am I going to do? The shareholders. The company. I can't do all this without her. We're completely unprepared."

Denise was having a meltdown. And though Colby continued to try to talk to her, the woman was unreachable. Emma stepped in. She tried consoling

Denise briefly, before clasping her shoulders and giving her a stern reorientation. "Listen, Denise. You need to think clearly. Focus on me! Look at me. I'm here! Everything's going to be all right. It will all work out. Just look at me. Okay?" Her grip on Denise's shoulders locked her in place.

Denise was in shock. Emma's quick thinking was able to bring Denise's emotions to a stable point but the damage had been done. She stared at the closed doorway again, as if the image of her aunt's body could still be seen. "I don't understand. What's happened? I'd just spoken to her on the phone last night."

Emma oriented Denise and helped her calm down some but not enough. Her own curiosity of the crime scene had caught Emma's eye but first Denise needed to exit the area. Emma distracted Denise's attention away from the doorway long enough to escort her with a bit of persuading back out to the front of the home. She used her grip on Denise to guide her outside. There was a chair on the large concrete porch and she had Denise settle into it. "Stay right here. The fresh air will help. Okay?"

Holding the door open, Emma made sure Denise was calm enough to leave alone for a moment. After several minutes, it seemed Denise had settled down enough. Before returning indoors, Emma spotted the men's two patrol cars parked up near the other side of the driveway. *Those weren't there earlier, were they?* Dismissing the thought, Emma made her way back inside and approached her father. The bedroom door stood open again, Colby and the Sheriff conveyed over the body on the bed.

"I think we should call the paramedics. Denise may still be in shock," Emma said as she stepped inside. "Do either of you know how long Denise was here?"

"The door was unlocked, so we came right in. The 10-39 we received this morning reported a body in the master bedroom," the Sheriff said.

Emma thought it strange that Denise left the door unlocked, but that maybe the security system was set up that way.

Colby gave the Sheriff a look of disdain. "You shouldn't see this, Emma, it's not good," Colby said. "Besides, you might be a risk to the integrity of the scene."

"I think I can help. Anyway, I'm not here for the body, I'm here for a cat. Dr. Lawrence told me to collect a cat," Emma rebutted.

"I haven't seen a cat around here," the Sheriff

said, kneeling down to look at the body from a different angle.

"Where's Gabby?" Emma asked Colby about his K9 partner.

"It's her day off. She's resting at the house," Colby replied, still frowning.

"Must be nice. Have you seen a cat?" Emma asked.

"Nope. No cats around here." Colby swiveled and took a quick look around to be sure.

Emma tapped a finger against her chin. *If Colby and Dad just arrived, who called in the death? For that matter, who called in that the cat needed to be picked up? Denise didn't seem as though she could have done it, and there hadn't been anyone else in the house that they'd seen yet.* It was all curious. She needed to find the cat but first she noticed something strange about the body in the bed.

CHAPTER THREE

Emma walked over to look at the body. Poor Mrs. Van Horn was soaking wet. Her night clothes were thoroughly covered in what looked like sweat. The area immediately around her body was also soaking wet. It was as if Mrs. Van Horn had drenched herself with several bottles of water whilst lying in the bed. Emma looked up to the ceiling for leaks but found none. The Sheriff eyed his daughter and smiled. "You notice it, too?"

"Is this much fluid normal for a heart attack?" Emma asked.

"I've seen it before, but this does seem like a lot. It's possible she may have evacuated during or after the attack," the Sheriff replied.

Remembering that Denise explained how the

house would automate the temperature, Emma was sure the deceased wouldn't have sweated to death. A heart attack seemed most likely. Poor Mrs. Van Horn.

"Normally heart attacks are more sudden, but it's possible that she suffered a wee bit. Regardless, I'm concluding heart attack, around three a.m. this morning," the Sheriff decided. "C'mon Colby, let's go interview the claimant and call in a 10-66." The Sheriff called out for George, the claimant.

Emma blinked as a man she hadn't seen yet came around the corner. Balding, stocky, and a little shorter than Emma, George wore a mask of concern. There was a definite family resemblance between George and Denise. The Sheriff introduced them. "This is a nephew of the decedent."

"Are you Denise's brother?" Emma asked.

"Cousin," he answered in a clipped tone, barely glancing up before his gaze dropped back down to the floor.

"Let's move this conversation to the living area, as I have a few questions for you as well, if you don't mind?" The Sheriff and Colby ushered George toward the living area so they weren't standing in the close quarters of the hallway. Emma followed, but kept her eyes open for the cat. The fake plants in the living room were a mixture of perennials, bamboo, and dracaena. Each was potted to look like real plants, with no dust on any of them. The entire house was well kept.

Emma's tingling nose alerted her to the possibility that a cat was nearby. She perked up, looking around the home from her vantage point in the living room. George was still explaining his story to Colby and the Sheriff but Emma's goals had not changed. Poor Molly waited in her SUV and she would need to check on the dog soon.

"My aunt had a late dinner meeting last night. She called me looking for a ride home because she'd had a bit too much to drink," George explained to the officers. "I dropped her off here at her house a little after 11 and had to help her get to bed. If I hadn't helped, she'd have forgotten to take her blood pressure medications, I'm sure."

"Once I left the mansion, on my way home, I got hungry and stopped for a quick snack at the convenience store just down the street from my townhouse."

Colby jotted down a note, probably to check for the alibi.

Emma observed Denise through the window, distraught and crying. George's behavior seemed quite calm and collected. *People react differently,*

Emma thought. In order to comfort Denise, Emma walked out to the front and invited Denise back into the house, advising her not to go into the master bedroom.

Denise agreed. Comforting her by wrapping her arms around Denise's shoulders, the two walked back in the house as George's interview ended.

Suddenly, Emma sneezed violently. Her allergies flared up. It had to mean the cat was close by. Her itchy eyes and runny nose were starting to irritate her. Emma looked around desperately trying to locate the feline.

George made finding it easy. The cat rubbed itself along his pants. "This darn cat always wants my attention," George said. Sneering at the tan and black long-haired cat, George flung his leg back and away from it.

"You know Julius has always liked you. How can you still hate cats?" Denise jabbed at George.

"Cats are so intrusive and selfish. They always take, take, take. Julius always wants me to pet him or feed him," George replied. "I'm much more of a dog person."

"That must be the cat Dr. Lawrence promised would be in the carrier." Emma sighed before sneezing again.

"Oh, I forgot to put Julius back in his box," George said, snapping his fingers. "This morning has been moving so fast. With everything that's happened, I totally forgot."

"That's fine. Can you get the transporter while I get the cat?" Emma asked.

"Julius doesn't like to be picked up." Denise grabbed Emma's arm, stopping her from fetching the cat.

"Well he needs to be in the tote, because I'm not driving back to the hospital with my allergies." Emma motioned toward George, "Would you please fetch the tote?"

The cat let out a soft meow in George's direction as he walked away. Emma decided to reach for the cat and sneezed again when she got close. Julius jetted across the house. "Well, shoot. This is going to be fun."

Julius perked up and stared down Emma, as if the cat knew a game of chase was afoot. As Emma neared, Julius would scurry away just out of reach. This game continued, all while Emma would sneeze any time she got close to the cat, encouraging it to run away faster each time. Eventually, the cat zoomed into the kitchen with Emma and Denise following behind.

The large dining room could seat at least twenty people. The dark oak table and maroon colored cloth gave an authentic Medieval but modern feel to it. On the table were place settings with very fine China, accompanied by polished silver cutlery and eating utensils. In the center of the table was a large vase, filled completely with wilted and dead flowers. The cat sat under the middle of the table.

"Maybe I should get him?" Denise offered.

"Yes, please. That might be for the best," Emma replied.

Denise began her attempt to collect the cat from under the table. It was unsuccessful. The excited feline sprung out from underneath the table, across the kitchen and back out into the foyer where George stood. He had not yet retrieved the cat carriage.

"This," Emma sniffled, "is going to be a lot harder than I thought."

"Julius will get tired before we do," Denise tried to joke.

The two began walking back to the foyer, when Denise tried apologizing to Emma for the dead flowers in the dining room. "I'm sorry you had to see those flowers. Normally my Aunt keeps this place fresh and vibrant all the time."

Emma eyed the flowers again.

"Actually, it's quite strange. The shareholders sent them over yesterday. They must not have been very healthy if they died overnight. But they also sent chocolates, so there's that," Denise said absent-mindedly as she followed Julius toward the foyer.

The Sheriff and Colby had made their exit during the fuss over the cat. They were outside waiting for the medical examiner to arrive. Emma saw them discussing something out front. "How nice of them to help," Emma mumbled with a frown.

"Where's the cat's travel box?" Denise asked when they arrived in the foyer.

"It's over there in the living room," George pointed. "On the other side of the plant next to the fireplace."

Denise marched off.

"Can you help me catch the cat, please? At least it likes you." Emma sniffled again. Her eyes were turning red from the allergies.

Grunting, George agreed. Emma took the small opportunity to take a look around. The box of chocolates sat on the foyer table. The bright red Valentine's Day box, shaped like a heart, proudly displayed the beautiful chocolates it should contain inside. *Maybe she could prolong her allergies with a chocolate*, Emma thought. She popped open the lid to sneak a caramel confection, finding the box to be a single melted box of chocolate. *There goes that idea*, she thought.

Denise returned with the tote just as George returned to the area, still following the cat. "The cat likes to play chase, but hates being picked up," Denise said to Emma.

"Does your cousin really hate cats?" Emma asked, glancing around at the framed artwork in the room. She noticed a few tiny rocks making a trail. Her eyes followed the trail to the litter box. *What a strange place to put the litterbox.*

"He doesn't like them because our Aunt likes them." Denise mentioned.

"What do you mean?" Emma asked, confused.

"Our aunt is always opposed to George. He wanted to do art, but she didn't think that was a good career path," Denise said.

George could hear them speak his name. "That's not true! I never liked cats from day one!"

"Maybe that's why the cat likes you," Denise teased, switching the tote between her hands.

George finally got ahold of the feisty feline, picking it up awkwardly and holding Julius out in front of him. "And my aunt never liked my art or my life choices." They fumbled with the cat to get it in the box. "She always said science was an art. She wanted all of us to follow her path and join the business." The cat finally gave in and got into the box. "I like my art more than security systems. It's freer." The plastic tote was quite tiny, but for the cat it was enough space to move around comfortably. "All right—one cat." George took the tote and handed it to Emma. "Here you go!"

"Our aunt really does want us all to join the business. I was going to ask her about moving up today, actually." Denise became visibly shaken. Emma wrapped her arm around her shoulder again while the girl looked down at the cat. "Will we be able to get him back?" Denise worried.

"Of course! The doc just wants to make sure the cat is okay, and to give the family time to grieve without having the responsibility of caring for an animal they're not accustomed to taking care of," Emma explained.

Denise's contorted face said she was holding back another emotional breakdown. Emma patted her on the shoulder.

"That makes sense," George said.

Denise nodded.

Emma sneezed, again, quickly turning away

from the group with the tote in her hands. "I should be going now. I have a dog in the car and I don't want to leave her long," Emma said. "But it's been nice meeting you both! This is a lovely home. I don't know why I've never stopped by here before."

"Thanks," George and Denise said at the same time.

"I wish we could be of more help," George suggested.

"I don't know what I should do now..." Denise muttered.

"Can you get back home?" Emma wondered.

"I could go home, but I need to let the shareholders know what happened," Denise said.

"That's a good idea," George nodded.

"I agree." Emma paused. "Spend some time with George, maybe call in to delay the meeting and collect your thoughts. Once you're prepared then go to the meeting," Emma suggested.

"I could go with you if you want. It's what she would have wanted," George said, wrapping an arm around his cousin.

"No, no. I can take care of it. The shareholders will look to me for updates anyway. They know you like your art more than the business," Denise said, pulling a tissue out of her purse and wiping her nose with it.

Emma watched them a moment, and then nodded. "I think that's a good plan. Let me take the cat and you two try to relax."

Emma went straight for her truck after nodding once more in farewell, her nose itching violently. Another sneeze was approaching.

Colby and her dad stood near their patrol cars that were parked next to Emma's SUV, talking about the events that had unfolded that morning. As she neared them, the sneeze came on full blast. The loud achoo startled Colby. "Goodness, girl! I thought you might blow a lung out there."

"I'll be..." She sniffled. "All right."

"Is that the cat?" the sheriff asked.

"Yes. Dr. Lawrence asked for me to get it and I did." Emma pulled a tissue from her jacket pocket and wiped her nose.

"Good job," her father said, eyeing her. "You look very nice today, by the way."

She smiled through her tearing eyes. "Thank you."

A glance at Colby showed her that her dad's suggestion had caused her crush to take notice of her, too. He eyed her outfit like he was seeing it for the first time. She only wished that the allergies weren't making it hard for her to appreciate the moment. She shook her head and tried to think of something else. "Oh yeah. Dad. I noticed the roses in the dining room were dead. George told me that they were just delivered yesterday."

"They probably forgot to water them or give them the nutrient packet. That kind of flower is very sensitive to this kind of humidity and temperature and without the right conditions any fluctuations would kill them fast," Colby said, glancing toward the house.

So, he noticed, too. Emma's affection for the man swelled in her chest.

"How are you able to speak more about flowers than any of the scenes we've been on?" the Sheriff asked.

"It's my mother's hobby, sir," Colby replied, a touch of pink colored his cheeks.

"Well, the flowers are dead," Emma continued. "But there was also a melted box of chocolates. Denise said the shareholders had the chocolates and the flowers delivered yesterday."

"That makes sense then, maybe the delivery truck left them out in the sun too long, or the cab was too hot, and they melted. It doesn't take long for chocolate to melt," Colby replied. His knowledge of the science amused Emma.

Her father grinned, equally amused. "Is that another hobby of yours? Mr. Chocolateer?"

"Just a hunch, sir." Colby replied, the pink in his cheeks growing.

Emma sniffed. "My allergies are flaring up. I need to get rid of this cat. Call me if you need anything."

"I will," said both the Sheriff and Colby.

The old man raised an eyebrow at Colby. "What reason would cause you to need to call my daughter?"

"It's Gabby, sir. I think the old girl has a cold. I might have worked her too hard outdoors the last few weeks." Colby rubbed his hands together as though they were cold.

Her father's amusement turned to concern as his forehead scrunched. "Uh huh. Well you just keep me up to date on your K9 partner. I don't want her missing too many days of work. It's bad enough she wasn't here for this case. I could have used her," the Sheriff said.

"Yes, sir," said Colby.

Emma smiled and opened the back door of her SUV. She set Julius on the back seat and looked through the bars toward the back of the vehicle at the Saint Bernard. "I'm so sorry, Molly. That took much longer than I expected. We'll let you get out of the truck when we get back to the vet hospital, okay?"

Molly's tail wagged as though she understood and forgave her. Emma shut the door and headed around to the driver's side, watching Colby and her father head back into the house with the medical examiner who had just arrived. As she sat in the driver's seat, she rolled the window down completely and blasted the fan of the car, trying to clear her sinuses as best as possible with the cat in the backseat. The unbearable itchy eyes and itchy nose was starting to fog her mind as well. She hoped it wouldn't impair her driving as she started back down the estate's driveway.

CHAPTER FOUR

The dozen minutes of severe cat allergies made the drive to the animal hospital quite agonizing. Emma wasn't sure if she'd take a job like this one again next time. Despite the hardship, she persisted knowing it wouldn't be long before she could clear up her lungs and get some proper fresh air.

Once inside the hospital, Dr. Lawrence received the cat carrier and expertly handled the locking mechanism. With one hand, the cage door was open, and Julius was instantly affectionate towards the vet. Dr. Lawrence's tall, thin frame was the opposite of George's, so it wasn't like the cat could have mistaken them, though they both had a deep timbre to their voices.

Maybe the cat likes men, she thought, remembering on the chase through the mansion earlier, and how quickly the cat showed the doctor some love.

The inspection procedure didn't take long, and the old man had his assessment within a few minutes. Emma was off in the corner trying to regain her breath after the allergy attack.

"Allergies, huh?" the old man remarked.

"Yep and this cat has been the worst for my nose. I couldn't breathe on the drive over." Emma snuffled as though her head were underwater.

"Well, if you ever get a cat, just make sure you bathe it regularly. Mrs. Van Horn brushed her cat regularly, but I can see she didn't bathe him as often. Your allergies come from the pet dander, oils, and the loose fur."

Somehow, Emma doubted she'd ever get a cat after today. "Thanks, I'll keep that in mind."

"This cat looks healthy, though. I don't see any issues here. Maybe a bath and another brushing and we'll have ourselves a precious little kitty! Won't we?" The old man's baby talk to the mature cat was a cute display of his affection for animals. It was a trait that Emma also shared, even with cats that sparked her allergies.

The old man started pawing at the cat, enjoying the play.

"What kind of cat is it? I still don't know all the breeds," Emma asked.

"This is a lilac point Himalayan. It's basically a cross between a Persian and a Siamese," he said.

"Great, so now I know not to go to the Himalayas from fear of my allergies." Emma joked.

"Nah, you'll be alright. These cats are rare in the wild, but they're definitely more of a house cat than an outdoor cat. Too much sun or heat is not good for any animal, but these..." He rubbed the cat's belly. "Are *definitely* indoor cats. They love their AC!"

"Gotcha. So, what now? Do I have to take him back?" Emma frowned at the thought. Julius was certainly adorable, and she'd love to play with him, but she'd had enough of him for one day.

"Oh no, he stays here with me until the owner comes for him," the doctor said.

"Well, unfortunately, Mrs. Van Horn passed away this morning. My dad thinks it was a heart attack." Emma relayed the message with a tone of sadness in her voice.

"I'm sorry to hear that," the doctor reminisced, "they didn't say she died when they called me this morning."

"Typical." Emma frowned eyeing Julius. "It's probably best if the cat stays here anyway. I'm sure the examiner would like some privacy."

"Oh certainly. When I..." Dr. Lawrence thought carefully about his words. "Never mind. Do you know if one of her heirs could come get the cat in a few days?"

"I'm sure George or Denise could, yea," Emma replied.

"Great. I'll just need one of them to sign the papers and we're all set." Dr. Lawrence's attention was solely invested in playing with Julius. The love that man had for animals was inspiring to Emma.

"Okay. Great. I'll see if I can't convince one of them to commit to get him in a few days and sign the papers," Emma said, her nose and eyes watering again. Dr. Lawrence's playfulness with the cat must have stirred up the air in the examination room. Emma could deal with a runny nose and the itchy eyes, but the pressure she felt in the back of her head was too much. "Do you need anything else?"

"Nope. Just give one of them a call for me and we're all set."

Emma nodded and headed out of the office. Once outside, she took deep, slow breaths of the open air as she approached her SUV. Her high heels were digging into her ankles and her toes hurt from walking in them all day. She opened the rear hatch for Molly, holding her leash, so the fur ball could stretch her legs. The morning had turned to afternoon. The poor Saint Bernard had been in the back of her car most of the morning.

"Sorry, again, Molly. I didn't mean for that to be the kind of day we'd have together." Emma closed the hatch and gave the puppy a good rub down. Then she led her toward the front of the vehicle.

Emma sat down in the driver's seat, ready to change out of her shoes. The agony of walking in heels was more uncomfortable than any comments she would receive for wearing sneakers with the skirt. Molly was ready to play and kept tugging at the leash to convince Emma to go to the play area next to the vet hospital.

"Just a minute, girl. I need to fix my feet first. Silly," Emma cooed at Molly.

She felt better once she had the tennis shoes on. It was smart of her to bring the extra footwear that day. She sighed, hoping that she wouldn't run into Colby again. But if he did say something, Emma thought of a few good one liners to change the subject quickly.

Letting Molly off the leash to run around the

play area, Emma stood idly by watching the dog prance around. Suddenly, a thought occurred to Emma. *Why is the cat okay, if the house was too hot? Would it have survived?*

She found her way back into the examination room, and caught Dr. Lawrence still playing with Julius. He had the stick with a string and a furry mouse on the end of it. Julius's curious eyes and pawing at the toy made her smile now that the pressure was gone from her head and she'd had a moment of fresh air.

"Hey, Dr. Lawrence?" Emma asked.

"Yes, dearie? Have you gotten ahold of an heir?" the doctor joked.

"No, I haven't asked yet. I was thinking about what you said... about the cats being indoor cats."

"Uh huh?" the doc was confused.

"Well, what would happen to a cat like this one," Emma nodded towards Julius, "if it were outside too long?"

"It's hard to say really, but cats are just like us. If I put you outside for too long in the summer sun, how would you feel?" The doctor was almost insulted.

"Well I mean, like what if it was temporary, and I brought it back inside after..." She thought a moment. "...after four hours?"

"Four hours? Four hours outside, in a hot sun? Are you an abuser? I would never—"

Emma cut him off. "What would the symptoms be?"

"Well a heart attack for starters. I'm sure dehydration would set in, liver failure, kidney failure, eventually leading to death. That's the cruelest thing you've ever asked me!" He looked at the cat again. "Is that what that old lady did to you? Huh? It's okay, you can tell me." The doctor began his inspection of Julius again under the impression Mrs. Van Horn was mistreating the animal. "He looks okay and doesn't appear dehydrated. Don't plant those ideas in my head, missy!"

"I'm sorry, Dr. Lawrence. I was just thinking about something, that's all. Don't worry! I would never leave my animals in the heat like that. That's cruel!" Emma was sure she had figured out a link between the chocolates, the flowers, and Mrs. Van Horn's sweating.

"You're certainly right that's cruel! They lock people in jail for that sort of thing!" The old doctor was getting hyped up about the idea that maybe someone would be cruel to an animal. It was good for Emma to see his enthusiasm for animal rights; it reinforced her ideas about them.

Emma headed back outside and observed the oblivious Molly still pandering around the yard. Her itchy nose had been reduced. Julius needed a signor to release him from the vet. Emma thought it would be a good idea to have Denise take the cat, since George didn't quite appreciate it as much. She didn't have Denise's number, so she called the station.

"Dispatch. Is this an emergency?" She blinked and looked at the phone. What was he doing answering the dispatch?

"Hi, Colby... it's Emma. Is my dad there?"

"Oh. Hi, Emma. No, he's not. I think he's on a patrol. The M.E. has already taken Mrs. Van Horn's body down to the morgue."

"Right, okay. Thanks for that. Do you have a phone number for Denise Van Horn? I'm trying to get one of the family members to sign for the cat, Julius?" Emma asked.

"Uh, yea sure. Hang on a sec." Colby could be heard putting the phone down. After a brief moment, he picked up again. "Hello?"

"I'm here." Emma's heart fluttered at the sound of his voice as he read off the phone number. She jotted it down. "Great, thanks. I appreciate it."

"No problem. How's your nose? You were pretty messed up earlier."

Her heart warmed at the concern in his voice. "It's all right now. That cat triggered my allergies pretty bad."

"I saw, I saw. Well, I hope you're fine now."

"Thanks, I'll be okay."

They said their goodbyes and hung up. Emma dialed Denise.

The line sounded distant and hollow. "Hello?"

"Hi Denise, it's Emma. I'm the one who picked up Julius this morning." Emma watched Molly as she dug a bit in the grass near a plastic fire hydrant.

"Hi Emma. What can I do for you?" Denise asked.

"I'm at the vet's office, and wondered if you might be able to stop in and fill out some paperwork for Julius?"

"Oh. I'm in the car right now, half-way to Richmond to talk to the shareholders. I won't be able to do that today... and I planned on staying overnight."

"Hmmm." Emma wondered if the vet's office minded waiting that long for the paperwork. She could ask Dr. Lawrence...

"You could ask George to do it. He's probably not busy." Her voice cut in and out slightly as the line was breaking up.

"Could I get his phone number from you?"

Emma asked, already pulling her car door open to grab her pen again. She wrote the number on her hand while Denise said them into the speaker phone. "Thank you."

"No problem. I'm nearly at my exit, so I'll let you go. Feel free to give me a call later if my cousin gives you a hard time."

"Thanks. And good luck at the shareholder's meeting."

Denise sighed. "Thank you. Talk to you later."

"Bye." Emma pressed the end call button and added Denise to her contacts. Then she dialed George.

When she asked if he could come fill out the paperwork, George explained, "Actually, my townhouse is at the other end of town and I'm expecting a package today. Would you mind bringing the paperwork over here and I'll sign it for you?"

Emma frowned. *People react differently*, she thought again. She agreed to meet him on the condition that he would be nice to the cat if he took possession of him. George agreed.

CHAPTER FIVE

Emma pulled up into the visitor's space immediately in front of the address George provided. Molly was still at the vet's in the play area. The poor dog was cooped up all day in the back of the car and Emma didn't want to do that sort of thing to her twice in one day.

On her walk to the front door, her foot stuck to a piece of gum. *Eww! Gross!* She used her car key to scrape off the waste. But as she continued her walk, the sound of ripping Velcro could be heard every other step. The sticky gum she removed must have been quite fresh.

"Still, better than heels," Emma murmured.

A moment after she knocked, George greeted her at the door and led her inside. The townhome was very disorganized. The man had stacks of computer parts, posters with brilliant designs, and all kinds of technology debris everywhere. Immediately, Emma's allergies started in motion. Her nose started itching and her eyes become red.

"Do you have a cat?" she managed to ask, before sneezing.

"No, I don't. But maybe it's because of my clothes. Let me change real quick," George replied. As he left to change, Emma started viewing the apartment as though it were an art gallery. The surplus of paintings and mixed digital artwork everywhere were extraordinary. The guy was talented. He had full pieces with only organic lines, and some with very stern contours. The colors were vibrant in some and muted in others. The black and white pieces were her favorite.

As she explored the paintings, the subjects of each changed between pieces. His muses seemed to come from many places. When she reached the corner of the room, her curiosity led her to shuffle through some of the mixed art leaning against the wall. As she moved through them, she dropped her pen.

He just needed the papers, I'm sure he already had a pen. Why did I bring a pen? Of course, I would drop it.

Upon retrieval of her pen, she found tiny rocks on the floor. They reminded her of the pebbles in the bottom of the fish tank she had as a young child.

Continuing her viewing session, each new piece reminded her of memories she had. The artwork was unlocking memories she hadn't thought about in a very long time. Each of the paintings had their own personality and use of color to covey mood. Emma picked up on his style immediately. She found a portrait of an old man and a young girl fishing off a pier. The perspective was from behind the two of them, and their bodies were silhouettes against the backdrop of the setting sun. The singular image reminded her so much of the relationship she and her father shared. It was beautiful.

Seeking more emotional pieces like that one, Emma browsed further. She stepped over a stack of computer equipment and found herself wondering if George had the kind of skills to hack his family's security system. *Surely he's not responsible. Was he? The artwork was quite voluminous... how could he have learned hacking skills?* The answer to the puzzle fit, though. George could have done it.

But what about Julius? Emma was confident she had found the solution, but the cat didn't make sense.

George returned to the living room in a new outfit. "Do you like my art work?"

"It's amazing. You did all of these?" Emma gestured to the pieces around the room.

"Yep. All me. I can't sell any of them, though." He bashfully looked away.

"Why's that? No buyers?"

"Oh no! No, no." George laughed. "I just feel like they're a part of who I am. I can't sell them. It would be like giving up a piece of myself."

"That's a shame. These are really good! Like, really *really* good. I would definitely enjoy seeing these in a gallery. They're breathtaking!"

"I'm glad you like them." George beamed.

"This one is my favorite." Emma reached towards the orange circle of the old man and the young girl.

"I call that one, 'Family.'" George's smile lit his face.

"How poetic. I love it." Emma grinned and set the portrait back.

"So, you have some paperwork for me, I presume?" George asked.

"I do, here." She handed him the three sheets of paper. "Dr. Lawrence said to sign here, here, and here." She pointed to the locations on the documents in rapid succession.

"Perfect. I'll be right back." George went into the other room, which Emma could only assume was intended as a dining room. The man had converted it into his studio. The computer setup and artwork all around that work area were even better than what he had on display in the living room.

"How can you make all of this beautiful art and not show the world?" Emma asked from the threshold to the kitchen.

"I can show you, if you like." He signed the last page and handed her the documents back. "Here, look." He opened up a tab on his computer. "Check this out." He pointed to the image previews of even more astonishing pieces stored digitally. "I couldn't handle the manual labor of painting, so I began digital work instead. My canvas is bigger, and I can get as detailed as I like."

"Have you shown these to anyone? They're incredible!" Emma expressed her amazement.

"Everyone that walks through that door." He laughed. "I show everyone my art, actually. I just don't sell them."

"I think you should, I know that people will buy these," Emma confidently suggested.

"Everyone says that, too!" They both laughed. When Emma sniffed and wiped her nose, he frowned. "Maybe it's not an allergy? I did change, I promise!"

"I mean, I guess it could be a cold. My head was a bit foggy earlier." Emma considered the possibility.

"A cold makes sense." George agreed. "Hey, if you want, I have chicken soup!"

"Oh, no. That's alright. I'll tough it out if it is a cold," Emma said. "What would you say if I told you I would buy that piece, 'Family,' I saw?"

"I'd say I appreciate the offer, and I'm glad you like it, but it's not for sale," George stated solidly.

"That's a shame. You wouldn't sell it for any amount that I would offer?" Emma liked the piece, but she would only really buy it if the price was low enough.

George sat silent, thinking for a moment. "I don't think I could, no."

"That's a real shame. You have so much potential with your skills! I've never seen art like this before. How did your aunt not approve of this?"

George's jaw tightened and his smile slipped from his face. His gaze darted to the left.

"She was a real stickler for the family business. She's also the reason you see all that computer garbage out here. Apparently, my apartment is a storage facility for the company. Since she paid the rent, she believed she could do with the place what she wanted." George grew agitated but took a deep breath and switched gears. "Let me show you some of my recent work. Everything you've seen so far was last years' works." He clicked through a few folders on the computer. Emma brushed her nose to try and get rid of the itch. "Check this out!"

On the screen was a scrolling array of photos, dozens of photos. They were just snapshots of larger images, but the crisp details, colors, subjects and styles were beyond belief. George could draw everything, real or imagined. Some of the pictures were so real in appearance, that Emma didn't believe he drew them. There were people and scenery, as well as architecture and buildings.

"These are all so amazing, George!" Emma knew the extent of his talent before, but the new works were next level. They were the art of the next generation.

"So, Emma?" George continued to look at the screen but his cheeks reddened. "I'm not really good at the whole social thing, so I'm just going to come out and ask. Would you like to be my valentine?"

She blushed, and blinked hard. "Oh, George. I'm sorry, but I've already made plans. Thank you for asking, though. It means a lot." Instinctively, Emma brought her thumb to her mouth and started nibbling on her nail. The worn-out nail was satisfying her anxiety over being asked by this strange guy, whom she'd only just met hours before, to be his valentine. It was too much.

Emma was nervous, hopefully not obviously nervous, as she stepped backward. *What was she doing alone in a house with a strange man?* She went through the checklist in her head. *Did anyone know she was here? Not really. Maybe Denise, but not really.*

"Really though, I appreciate you showing me your artwork. You're super talented! But I need to get back to the hospital to deliver these documents before they assume he's abandoned and send Julius to the shelter. I appreciate everything!" She held the papers close to her chest and rushed over to the door where he saw her out. She wasn't listening when he said goodbye. The brisk walking pace to her car caused a slight slip from the shoe with the gum on it. George had already closed the door and didn't see. He'd turned cold once she'd turned him down. Maybe she'd hurt his feelings.

She couldn't breathe freely again until she was sitting in the driver's seat of her SUV. Instinctively, she locked the doors and took deep breaths. *What a weirdo. He likes you. Why would he ask you out like that? Is he lonely?* Dismissing her anxious thoughts, Emma slipped off her shoe to clean the gum permanently. The dog bag in the backseat had some moist wipes which Emma grabbed.

As she began cleaning the shoe, the same tiny pebbles from the house were popping off of the bottom of her shoe. Her nose started itching and the teary eyes returned immediately upon smelling the scented rocks. Then everything fell into place in her mind.

Her heart lurched in her chest.

CHAPTER SIX

"Dad, listen, I know you have a habit of not believing me, but I don't think Mrs. Van Horn died of a sudden heart attack." Emma's bursting excitement exhilarated her while she spoke on the cell with her dad.

"Sweetie, slow down. You know I can't hear through these phones very well," her father said.

"Okay. Okay. I'm sorry. I'll try to contain myself. Look, remember the cat? Julius?" Emma started rushing her words again and caught her breath.

"Yea. What about it? Are you still having an allergic reaction?"

"No, I'm fine. I mean, yes." She took a breath, sniffling. "But that's not the point. My allergies are what solved the case!"

"I don't understand, honey. You're going to have to lay it all out for me."

"Do you remember at the house when we were chasing the cat around?"

"I can't say I do, no."

"Right, okay. Well, while you and Colby were out front we had to chase Julius around the house." She continued sitting in her SUV, while watching the front of George's townhouse. She was afraid he might check on her through the curtain but to her relief, it never moved.

"Okay." He paused to let her continue.

"Well, when we got into the kitchen, there were some flowers on the table. And they were wilting. Remember I told you?"

"Right, that's what you said when you came out of the house."

"And Colby said that maybe they weren't watered. But then I brought up the chocolates?"

"Right, and the idea was maybe they weren't delivered in the best condition. It's all plain, sweetheart," her father said, but his tone said she was tiring him.

"No, it's not! Listen, this is what I'm trying to say. I think George is some kind of hacker or something, I don't know. But I don't think I'm allergic to the cat. I think I'm allergic to the litter from the litterbox." Emma exhausted her breath speaking so fast.

"Really? That's an interesting discovery." He had started sounding condescending now.

"Dad, no, wait. I mean that I think George hacked into the house somehow. He changed the temperature in the house to sweltering hot. Then cooled it back down again. His aunt has a heart condition. It's why the chocolates were melted and the flowers wilted. The only thing that didn't make sense was Julius. Julius would have died too, if he had been in the house. But he wasn't in the house. He was at George's. There's litter at his house. He doesn't have a cat."

"That's a compelling argument, honey, but I don't think it's enough for a warrant."

"But if you get a warrant and search his computer, I'm sure you can find solid evidence for conviction. I'm telling you, Dad, I saw the same litter at the house as in the townhome. I'm sitting in the parking lot in front of his house right now. And my allergies wouldn't lie!"

"Okay, it couldn't hurt to pass it through the judge. Hang tight, and get out of that parking lot until we get there, okay?"

"Okay, dad. I love you."

"I love you too, sweetie."

Emma moved her car away from the row of townhomes just out of sight of George. *Maybe I spent too long in front of his house. Does he know that I know?* She had to calm herself. Molly would have been a huge help to her anxiety in that moment but Molly was still at the vet. She definitely needed to look into making Molly a therapy dog. The Saint Bernard puppy was already providing her with all kinds of therapy relief.

Breathe in. Emma told herself and took a deep breath. *Breathe out.* She exhaled.

Breathe in. Emma told herself again and took another deep breath. *Breathe out.* She exhaled. Her thumb nail found its way to her mouth again, slowly being whittled away by her teeth. *This is taking too long.*

The phone ringing startled her and she almost knocked the SUV into drive. Her dad was calling.

"Hello?" Emma answered.

"Em? Hi honey. Everything's all set. We're having two units sent to the complex now, Colby and I will be in one of the cars. Just sit tight."

"Okay. Don't worry, I'm not moving."

"Atta girl. Just stay where you are, and don't go back into the townhouse."

"Oh, you don't have to worry about that," She laughed.

"I love you, and good work. I'm proud of you!"

"Thanks Dad, I love you."

CHAPTER SEVEN

Colby and the Sheriff arrived first on the scene. Emma flagged them down and together they headed up to the apartment door. George greeted them at the door, his face a mask of confusion. His eyes darted toward Emma and then the two officers. "What's this about?"

The Sheriff cleared his throat and presented the search warrant. "We have a warrant to search your town home, Mr. Van Horn."

George paled and blinked several times, his brow suddenly growing clammy. "I don't understand. Why?"

"Allow us inside, Mr. Van Horn, if you please, and we'll explain."

Shocked, George stepped to the side and allowed

the three of them entry. Confusion clouded his features as he closed the door behind them and stood in the foyer to hear her father speak.

"My daughter, Emma here, is somewhat of an amateur detective. Her allergies are what led us to suspect your involvement in Mrs. Van Horn's death."

George blinked again and then he laughed. His gaze slid past Emma's as though avoiding hers. He headed toward the kitchen. "I think I need a drink. Anyone else need anything?"

They all politely declined. Colby surveyed the apartment with his hands in his pockets, while Emma followed the Sheriff toward the kitchen.

"So, you're saying that your daughter had an allergic reaction in my house and somehow that means I killed my aunt? Sounds a bit crazy if you ask me. Are you sure your daughter doesn't need to see a therapist." His eyes danced with mirth as he took a sip from the soda can he just popped open.

A pinprick of hurt sliced through Emma's chest. Emotionally, she wanted to lash out and defend herself but she needed to be rational. He was a murder, she was certain. And right now, he was deflecting. If he could convince everyone that she was crazy in her accusation, he would get away with murder. She tilted her head. "If you don't have a cat, why do you have kitty litter in your apartment?"

He coughed as he choked a bit on his soda. "What are you talking about?"

The sheriff stepped forward. "Do you have any cats, sir?"

"No, Sheriff. I don't own any cats. But I did change clothes when Emma was here earlier. We thought and agreed together that maybe the cat hairs on my clothes were the issue causing her allergies."

"Right, I understand that. But did you have kitty litter on your clothes?"

"No. I don't think so." George looked down around the floor near his chair.

"Honey, would you care to explain?" the Sheriff asked Emma.

"Gladly. So, when we were at your aunt's house, I saw the litter box in the foyer. It was strange, but not something I would have thought to be an issue. What didn't add up was the spilled litter next to the box. I initially thought the cat may have just made a mess and it hadn't been cleaned up since Mrs. Van Horn had already succumbed," Emma explained.

"That doesn't explain why we're in my apartment right now," George smugly suggested.

"I was getting to that. When I took the cat to the vet, my allergies were just as bad as they were at your aunt's mansion. They started to clear up once I deposited the cat, so I didn't think much of it." She took a breath. "When I came to your apartment, my allergies had been dormant until I got inside. You suggested it was the cat hair and I bought into the idea. Unfortunately, you forgot something."

"My underwear?" George tried to joke, but not even he laughed.

"The kitty litter. Obviously used kitty litter has cat remnants, which could also spark an allergic reaction, which it did for me. You then suggested I might have a cold. You had me convinced. It wasn't until I got in my car that I realized I had kitty litter stick to my shoe. My reaction flared up again."

"I don't understand. Couldn't you have gotten the litter on your shoe from my Aunt's house?" George glared at Emma trying to back her into a corner with that question.

Colby perked up and even the Sheriff held his breath. "Not possible. I changed my shoes at the vet. I was wearing heels earlier. When I arrived at your apartment, there's no other way for me to have gotten kitty litter on them, especially since the gum outside caused it to stick to my shoe."

"But that doesn't prove anything. Maybe there's kitty litter outside?" George rebutted.

"Could be. But I know there's litter here in the house." Emma pointed to the corner of the room. Colby immediately went over to look.

"I can confirm, we have little rocks," Colby said from his kneeling position in the corner.

"You brought the cat home last night, hacked the security system, cranked up the heat and killed your Aunt."

"No way. Her symptoms showed she died of a heart attack. Ask the Sheriff."

"It was a heart attack, sweetie. The Medical Examiner confirmed it."

"See?" George looked smug.

"Then explain the dead flowers and the melted chocolates, George."

George blinked but the shocked look on his face faded instantly into disinterest. "The chocolates melted? What chocolates?"

"Yes, the chocolates melted. The chocolates the shareholders sent to your aunt yesterday. I took a look in the box because I wanted one. The whole tray had melted into a solid piece." Emma argued. "You cranked up the temperature. The computer technician will be here shortly to check your computer for evidence."

His face tensed and he glared at the soda can in his hands.

Emma continued, "The overwhelming heat caused your aunt's heart attack after you left. It must have been on a while, at least three or four hours, because she lost a lot of water weight. More than normal. She probably had a heart attack due to the dehydration. Or maybe it was the sudden temperature change when you cooled the house back down. But you saved the cat. You hated your aunt, but you're not a bad guy, are you, George? You still saved the cat because you didn't want to see someone innocent die."

George's face twitched. His jaw clenched and unclenched. "My aunt wasn't innocent. She was a monster. She treated me like garbage. I wasn't sure that hacking into the system would kill her. I just wanted her to suffer a little bit."

"But you had to know that she might die."

He shrugged. "She might get sick, she might die. Either way was fine with me."

"Mr. Van Horn, I'm placing you under arrest for the premeditated murder of Mrs. Van Horn." The Sheriff continued to read off George's rights and began to handcuff the poor guy.

"You see that flash drive there?" George asked and Colby went for it. "It's got the hack I used to break the system. Don't let that out of your sight. It's my whole family's livelihood."

"The fact that it exists will be public record, Mr. Van Horn, but the contents can remain confidential. Don't worry, it's safe," Colby said.

"I don't want to hurt the business. This was personal between me and my Aunt."

"Because she hated your artwork?" Emma asked.

"Because she never believed in me at all. She resented me because I rejected the family business," George said with a sad smile. The Sheriff hauled him off to his patrol car.

As they were starting out the doorway to follow her dad, Colby turned to Emma, and looked deep into her eyes. Her heart raced in her chest. It was as though he was really seeing her as something other than a fourteen-year-old kid for the first time. "Emma, I don't know what to say. You're like a modern Sherlock Holmes."

Emma laughed, casting her glance down to hide the blush. "I don't think I'm Sherlock. Not yet anyway."

"Really, that was amazing detective work. Why haven't you joined the force?" Colby asked.

She shrugged one shoulder. "I like animals. They're comforting. There's just something about them that I enjoy more."

"You could do the K9 unit, like I do." Colby suggested as they stepped to the side to allow the rest of the police force into the apartment to search for more clues.

"I'll think about it. It sounds fun, but I don't think that's what I'm destined to do."

"Well, I'm off work now. This was my last task for the day. I don't know how your dad works so many hours. He's a machine."

"He's divorced. Work is his way of coping. Are you going to go see Gabby?"

"Gabby's all right. She's resting at home. Her day off. Lucky dog." He pulled off his cap and scrubbed his hand through his sandy brown hair.

The movement mesmerized Emma for a moment. "Yea, lucky, huh?"

"Have you eaten yet?"

Emma's heart leapt. She shook her head but inside, she was screaming.

"Have dinner with me and Gabby?"

She swallowed down the hormones, hoping that Colby wouldn't see her as that fourteen-year-old girl again. She tried to sound as mature as possible as she asked, "Are you cooking?"

He laughed. "If buying take-out is cooking, then yes. I'm cooking. But you have to do the driving."

They both shared a giggle. Emma's heart was bursting in her chest. "I have to pick up Molly at the vet's first, but you have a deal."

CHAPTER EIGHT

The sunset off in the distance colored the sky a deep orange and purple. Emma felt a chill in the air as the temperature was falling. The stars found their way over the east horizon, as she, Colby and Molly sat in the SUV. They changed plans and got dinner at a drive-in on the way to Colby's house.

"It's gonna be a cold night, tonight." Colby smiled and took a bite out of his burger.

"But look at all the stars!" Emma was peering out of her window at the sky. "I wish this fast food place would let us have dogs in there."

"I'm sure one day they might." He laughed around another bite.

"Here, Molly." Emma fed a few french-fries to

the Saint Bernard. When she turned back around, she saw Colby's eyes in a new light. His green eyes were darkened by the sunset but they were showing concern.

"You know, when I got the call to go to the townhouse, I thought you were in danger. I got worried." Colby's forehead wrinkled and he chewed a bit on his bottom lip.

"I was fine; I sat in my car away from his place."

"You need to be safe about those sorts of things; you can't just go off and meet a stranger like that alone. Not if it's related to a case we're working on."

"I'm sorry." Emma stopped nibbling on her hamburger.

"It's okay, it's a mistake. But the guy turned out to be a murderer. That's not a safe situation to be in."

"Yea, that was pretty crazy," Emma admitted.

The setting sun basically meant Valentine's was ending. And she'd got to spend the ending of it with him. Inside, she gushed. Then she thought about Colby's advice.

He cares about me. He didn't want me to get hurt. He thought I was in danger.

She loved that he cared. She took a huge bite of her sandwich to hide the smirk on her face.

Molly woofed, and Colby said, "All right, fine, here's another french-fry. Greedy."

Emma laughed, enjoying their company. That moment was the best Valentine's Day present ever.

The End

Look for more of Emma and Molly's adventures:
http://amazon.com/author/pcreeden

MURDER ON VALENTINE'S DAY

IT'S NEW YEAR'S EVE AND 20-YEAR-OLD EMMA WRIGHT HAS A DATE WITH HER crush—well, not a real date, but she can dream! Colby Davidson, the K9 search and rescue deputy, is allowing her to accompany him while he's on patrol at the Ridgeway Illumination Festival. Though they are just friends, she's still hoping for a possible kiss at the end of the festivities.

When a stranger asks them to help take some pictures at the event, Emma and Colby are happy to oblige. But their assistance turns them into alibis for the man's whereabouts while his girlfriend was killed. Most of the clues point to a robbery gone bad, but Emma doesn't believe all of them point that way. Was it really a robbery or was it murder?

It's Valentine's Day and 20-year-old Emma Wright just wants her crush to take notice of her. But Colby Davidson, the K9 search and rescue deputy only thinks of her as a kid sister. How will she get him to take her seriously?

When her veterinarian boss calls her to pick up a cat at a potential crime scene, she finds herself at the house of the richest woman in Ridgeway. Her father—the sheriff—and Colby are there. They both dismiss the untimely death as a heart attack, but Emma finds clues that it might be something more. Did the software billionaire die of natural causes, or was it murder?

It's St. Patrick's Day and 20-year-old Emma Wright is working hard at training five-month-old Molly, her foster puppy, to become a therapy dog. But her training coach and neighbor gets an emergency call, cutting the lesson short, and Emma volunteers to pick up her daughter at a St. Patrick's Day concert in town.

When Emma arrives, the concert has just finished up, and the teenage girls are visiting with the band. Then the lead singer stumbles and falls to the ground, dead. Emma becomes the only level head in the crowd and calls for help. When the Sheriff and Colby arrive, they investigate it as a potential accident. But Emma finds subtle clues that something more sinister is going on. Did the leader of the band die in an accident, or was it murder?

All hands on deck! It's a beautiful spring day and 20-year-old Emma Wright is meeting her crush, Colby Davidson, for a two-hour tour specifically for dogs and their owners – *The Canine Cruise*. She and Molly, the Saint Bernard, are so excited to see both Colby and Gabby, his K9 partner, as the two have been away on training.

It's smooth sailing until someone shouts "man overboard!" A news reporter who is covering the day cruise for a local station falls into the fast-flowing Potomac River, and she doesn't know how to swim. Did the reporter fall overboard in an accident, or was it murder?

Coming in May: Emma and Molly attend a wedding... where a murder overcomes the romance of the occasion!

ABOUT THE AUTHOR

If you enjoyed this story, look forward to more books by P. Creeden.
In 2019, she plans to release more than six new books!
Hear about her newest release, FREE books when they come available, and giveaways hosted by the author—subscribe to her newsletter:
https://www.subscribepage.com/pcreedenbooks
All subscribers also get downloadable copy of my PUPPY LOVE coloring book.

If you enjoyed this book and want to help the author, consider leaving a review at your favorite book seller – or tell someone about it on social media. Authors live by word of mouth!

Made in the USA
Monee, IL
27 March 2023